SANCTUARY 101

CONNOR WHITELEY

No part of this book may be reproduced in any form or by any electronic or mechanical means. Including information storage, and retrieval systems, without written permission from the author except for the use of brief quotations in a book review.

This book is NOT legal, professional, medical, financial or any type of official advice.

Any questions about the book, rights licensing, or to contact the author, please email connorwhiteley@connorwhiteley.net

Copyright © 2024 CONNOR WHITELEY

All rights reserved.

DEDICATION
Thank you to all my readers without you I couldn't do what I love.

CHAPTER 1

A thousand holy women missing without a trace.

Sister Superior Scarlett Evans leant against the boiling hot sandstone wall of the monastery staring out into the wasteland beyond. She was grateful for the loud hum of her armour's cooling systems working overtime to make sure the sheer, extreme heat from the outside didn't bother her.

The endless wasteland was a blurry haze from the heat of the world and Scarlett was glad she wasn't a mere Battle Sister these days. She didn't want to be in charge of scanning and making sure she could see everything that was coming or not towards them.

The immense ring of dunes in the distance looked almost like a mountain range the size of the Alps on Old Earth. Scarlett was sure there were mountains or something solid on this world but she couldn't see it.

The entire wasteland just looked like an endless blanket of yellow sand with dunes rising in the distance. And deep slashes in the distance to her right, she didn't want there to be a sandstorm because again, that would only cause problems for the scanners.

Scarlett coughed as she got an intense dry, acrid gust that smelt so foul and hot that it sucked even more moisture from her body. She hated how the air felt like it was trying to kill her.

She didn't want to be out here much longer because clearly her equipment wasn't good enough to last out here, but she wanted to bear witness to what her sisters had seem.

Yet at least the sky was crystal clear. It made it easy to see any incoming enemies, and she could see the comforting sight of the metallic blue blade-like warships of her legion. The Sirens of Ares.

She liked being a superhuman Angel of Death and Hope helping her friends and the divine Lord of War conquer humanity and free it from the chaos of the Great Human Empire.

The Empire might have seen her as a traitor that wanted to enslave humanity, but that wasn't true. She simply wanted to help humanity live safely under the religious doctrines of her Lord and Master.

A single bead of sweat rolled down her forehead.

She had already read the environmental reports when she was in orbit yesterday and she never wanted to be outside unprotected. The planet *Sanctuary* was so hot, a person might be boiled before they could even scream out in utter terror, or maybe even realise what was happening.

But this was the Lord of War's divine Will. He wanted her and her sisters to be here so she was going to be no matter what happened to her.

Scarlett felt the rough sandstone behind her back and she hissed as a piece broke off and jabbed into her back. The entire monastery was abandoned, lost and all one thousand of her sisters were missing.

That was why she was here.

Scarlett took a few more steps away from the wall and looked back at the immense sandstone wall. It wrapped itself around the entire monastery like it could withstand anything like bombs, orbital bombardment and whatever a ground assault could unleash on it.

That was normally true because the impressive and advanced shielding and other faithful technology her legion had access to, but clearly all the technology had failed.

Now that sandstone wall was all sliced, slashed and lashed up like a child had gotten a red hot knife and stabbed it into butter over and over and over.

Scarlett didn't know what it would take to annihilate the holy wall for good, but it wouldn't take much. Maybe a single bullet, maybe a simple breath, maybe not even that.

Beyond the sandstone wall, Scarlett shook her head at the perfectly intact massive box-like monastery that looked like the most stunning piece of art she had ever seen. It was easily the size of a skyscraper, large enough to fit an immense small town inside and the stained-glass windows were simply stunning.

All Scarlett wanted to do was go inside and explore the ancient halls and admire all the stunning red, purple blue stained glass windows of the Lord of War, her Legion Lord and all the amazing victories they had gained since their founding.

Yet most of all, she simply wanted to find out what had happened to her sisters.

Including her blood sister.

Scarlett blinked ten times as her eyes watered at the very idea of her sister, Jade. They had both been "kidnapped" (more like rescued) by the Sirens of Ares when they were 5 years old and taken away from their toxic, abusive backwater world of a home and raised with love, respect and power by the Sirens.

Scarlett had loved reading to Jade, making up grand stories of adventures and saying that they could travel the stars together as a team. They could kill the Empire, their abusers and they could save all the other small children that the Empire didn't care about.

Jade had been a lot more devout than Scarlett ever was but Scarlett was proud of her sister. She commanded respect and influence throughout the entire legion, so it was a little odd she got posted on an isolated world like Sanctuary but Jade had always said she was here because it was what the Lord of War willed.

Scarlett wasn't going to argue with that.

When news had reached her five years ago that Sanctuary had stopped transmitting and reporting to Command, Scarlett hadn't wanted to believe Jade was in danger or worse.

Jade was probably just too busy praying, leading her sisters into battle or doing something else entirely. She was always devout like that.

But as Scarlett stood in front of the lashed, slashed and crumbling sandstone wall in front of Sanctuary 101, she knew that wasn't the case.

Something that had happened here to Jade and 999 other sisters that happened so quickly they couldn't report it, they couldn't fire a shot and they couldn't escape.

Or maybe they did.

Scarlett hadn't seen any bodies yet but that didn't mean they weren't here somewhere. Or maybe Jade was alive and well. Her sweet little sister might be alive, and Scarlett just hoped that was true.

And as the immense roar of metallic blue blade-like fighters screamed overhead, Scarlett smiled because her sisters were coming and now she had back-up she could finally start to explore Sanctuary 101.

Something that both terrified and excited her in equal measure.

CHAPTER 2

Lady Madeline flat out couldn't understand why the hell she of all people had been "gifted" this crappy little assignment. She was a Black Claw, a spy, assassin and investigator that reported to the Lord of War himself. She was used to spying on superhuman legions, assassinating governors that were questioning if they should return to the Empire or not, and she was an enforcer of the Lord of War's will.

This mission was beneath her, and she hated the Sirens of Ares with a passion.

"We'll land in a moment my Lady," a computerised voice said.

Madeline stood in the middle of a large metallic blue box-like transport compartment surrounded by the constant banging, humming and vibrating of the blade-like shuttle's engines.

The transport compartment wasn't that bad and at least it smelt refreshing of oil, lavender and holy incense that the damn Sirens of Ares seem to burn obsessively. All the metallic blue surfaces were smooth, shiny and almost sterile except for the sooty substance thinly covering the walls because of the sheer amount of incense burnt.

Madeline didn't want to complain too much and she forced herself not to give anything away. Especially given now there were ten Sisters in their dirty, dented metallic blue superhuman armour sitting only metres from her.

Their armour was the typical Mark 9 type styled on that of the Knights of Old Earth. Madeline rather liked Mark 9 armour and she always enjoyed wearing the enhanced version. It made her feel so powerful, strong and like she could rip through an entire army with her bare hands.

She might have "only" been a baseline human without any of the fancy upgrades, organs and superhuman abilities of the Angels, but Madeline never wanted to upgrade. She was a Black Claw and sometimes being a baseline human helped her and opened a hell of a lot more doors than the Angels could ever realise.

All of the Angels she killed or spied on never thought she was dangerous.

And she hoped this Sister Superior Scarlett Evans would be the same.

The humming, banging and vibrating of the engines got even louder for a moment as Madeline felt the shuttle bank a little and the temperature rose dramatically.

She looked at the Angels who didn't seem to notice. Madeline hated the feeling of sweat rolling down her back and forehead and her throat felt like a desert. She had read about the extreme heat of Sanctuary but this was unreal.

"My Lady," a female Angel said behind her but Madeline couldn't tell which one, "you must put on your protective gear before we climb,"

Madeline nodded. "Do you not worry about me Angel. I will be fine but thank you for your concern,"

She reached into the pocket of her long black trench coat and pulled out a small circular disc and activated it. Madeline never wanted to deny or not use the cool equipment the Lord of War gifted his Black Claws.

The temperature fell around her to a more manageable level and her throat stopped feeling like it was a desert slowly seizing up. But the extreme heat of Sanctuary was going to be important information for sure, she might be able to turn the planet's weather into a weapon against the Sisters if needed.

An idea she definitely wanted to try out if needed.

Madeline subtly reached up to the blue glassy symbol on a golden chain around her neck. She liked how icy cold it felt in her hand and she was glad to have the full weight of the Lord of War's authority behind her.

If anyone tried to kill her, stop her or do anything against her mission then it was basically treason. And as much as her necklace closed doors to her, she was glad to have it when dealing with the Sirens of all people.

Most of the legion saw her as a prophet or demi-god because she had actual regular contact with their so-called divine being. There were a few that saw her for what she actually was.

But thankfully those bright souls were few and far between.

A strong whiff of overwhelming incense made Madeline cough a little and she was so looking forward to being done with the damn Sirens of Ares. She hated listening to their prays, their services and reading their stupid doctrines about the Lord of War. He was no God but their belief made them easy to control.

The only comfort she was taking from this situation.

As far as she was concerned the Sirens were zealots that murdered for no reason, like they murdered her twin brother Charlie for no reason. He was a Black Claw like her, they were in the middle of a massive battlefield where everything was going wrong, and then the damn "traitors" they were fighting alongside surrendered to the Empire.

Lady Madeline still felt the burn and lump in her lower back from a bullet she got during that battle.

When the damn "traitors" had surrendered to the Empire, her and Charlie had just wanted to run and flee with their prize. A lot of Republican Credits, new advance weapons and genetic material for experimentation.

The Sirens had disagreed.

Lady Madeline subtly rubbed her lower back as the bullet burnt with searing pain for a brief moment.

The Sirens had unleashed every single weapon, missile and bomb they had on the "traitors" because they did not want their warships falling into the hands of the Empire.

Charlie was on one of those ships so he died. All because the Sirens didn't want to displease their God and risk some future threat even though all the mission parameters were done.

She hated them and she was going to make the Sirens pay no matter the cost.

"Landing now," another Angel said.

Madeline nodded. She just needed to be in their company a little longer, find out what happened to the Sisters and make sure the Lord of War's hands were kept clean. The Lord of War had only told her 3 things about the events of Sanctuary 101.

It was no accident, the Empire hadn't been involved and the truth had to remain hidden.

Madeline had no idea what to make of it but considering this was the only expedition licensed to come and investigate on Sanctuary, she just wanted to make sure that Scarlett and her sisters died here after they had helped her find the truth.

The shuttle banged and jerked and popped as it landed.

Bright blinding light shone into the transport compartment as the wall in front of her lowered and Madeline just grinned because she was finally on Sanctuary and she had a mission to do.

She saw Sister Superior Scarlett standing there in front of the lashed, slashed and sliced-up sandstone wall. She looked surprised standing there in her bright metallic blue armour but there was a hardness to her look.

Scarlett wouldn't be an easy woman to deal with and Madeline didn't have a problem with that. Scarlett was still a Siren of Ares and that meant she could use her authority and her connection to the Lord of War to control her, or at least turn her dumb sisters against her.

That would be enough and Madeline was so looking forward to their games beginning.

And she looked forward to killing the sisters and Scarlett even more.

CHAPTER 3

Scarlett had absolutely no idea whatsoever why there was a bloody Black Claw here. She hadn't noticed Lady Madeline on the ship, in any official communication and she had no idea how she was here in the first place.

Not that it mattered now.

After Madeline had introduced herself, her authority and her "purpose" (some crap about observing the most holy Sisters so the Lord of War could reward them) to all one hundred Battle Sisters that had come down on the transports, Scarlett had led them inside the monastery.

Scarlett stood in the immense nave on the ground floor of Sanctuary 101 that was immediately behind the massive solid steel domed door. It was incredible to see all the thousands upon thousands of tiny little figures of saints, Legion Lords and Battle Sisters carved into the steel.

She was just grateful that the monastery naturally

seemed to keep the extreme heat out. Her and her sisters didn't have to have their helmets on so she could see the beautiful monastery with her natural, superhuman sight without the technological filters and data feeds interrupting the holy sight.

Scarlett had no intention of going back out in that heat for as long as she could help it.

Even the nave was stunning with its immensely tall domed ceiling made from polished white marble with blue, gold and purple veining through it. Scarlett was even more impressed the marble ceiling had been crafted in such a way that the veining depicted grand battles that the legion had fought since the founding of the Sisterhood.

On the ceiling of the nave showed the very first battle the Sisterhood had been involved in after they had declared the Emperor to be a false God.

An immense space battle with thousands of Empire and "Traitor" warships scattered through the ceiling with artful blue and purple veining showing the explosions of cannon fire and laser discharge.

Scarlett had never seen a more beautiful ceiling.

Even the gigantic perfectly straight orange, pink and yellow sandstone walls were impressive with thousands of small arches carved into them by hand. In each arch there was a small handmade candle that every sister made as a show of dedication to the Lord of War.

Scarlett loved the rituals of her sisters, because every single night before when her sisters, including

Jade, were here, each candle was lit in hope of guiding the faithless towards their purpose as servants of the Lord of War.

The sound of her sisters gasp, mutter prays and quietly sing divine songs made Scarlett smile. The dirty metallic blue of her sisters was a great contrast and it was lovely to feel alive in a creepy and mysterious place like Sanctuary 101 where everything seemed perfect on the surface.

That was the problem.

All the candles were perfectly intact, unlit and unburnt.

Scarlett shook her head as she realised that everything in the nave was in perfect condition as if Sanctuary 101 had been finished yesterday. There were no marks of wear or time on the sandstone walls and the ceiling was beyond perfect.

Even the polished black marble floor was in perfect condition that was impossible. Scarlett had been to tens upon tens of holy places over her career and there were always chips, marks and wear-patterns in the floor. It was simply a hazard of the faithful.

This nave was basically new and Scarlett couldn't understand that.

Scarlett smiled at the idea of Jade being here exploring the nave and halls and towers of this entire place. Jade would have loved singing and leading her Sisters in their prays and making Sanctuary 101 feel like the centre of their Faith.

Scarlett wished she was more like Jade, because

Jade was amazing, caring and she could rally entire towns of unfaithful to her cause if the need arose. That was how brilliant Jade was.

She had to find out what happened to her sister.

"Sister Superior," a tall Angel called Sophie said, "we have completed our initial scans and whilst there is too much interference because of the approaching sandstorm, we are confident we are alone,"

Scarlett nodded. Sophie had always been a brilliant Sister, she was devout, cunning and Scarlett didn't doubt she could kill anything with the right tool. So Scarlett didn't doubt the interference was real and not some rookie error.

"Thank you, Sister. Please look around, enjoy the space and prepare for the Service tonight," Scarlett said.

She had no idea what she was going to tell her Sisters but they were the first Sirens back here in so long that it only felt right to add some holiness to the violated place.

Scarlett looked around and noticed that the damn Black Claw was leaning against the closed steel door like she owned it. Lady Madeline looked so arrogant, stupid and weird just standing there in her black trench coat and that terrifying blue eye symbol hanging around her neck.

A small part of Scarlett wanted to mutter a pray, worship or even pay respects towards the necklace because it was the symbol of her Lord and Master. But she was never going to show Lady Madeline that sort of respect, Scarlett would rather die.

Little did she realise just how likely that option would be.

Scarlett wanted to shout at Lady Madeline for daring to lean on the door and risk damaging the carvings on the door but then she noticed what Lady Madeline was actually doing.

She was studying them.

Lady Madeline was watching all of them with her narrow eyes and Scarlett had never seen someone look at her sisters with such intensity and possibly hate before. She knew her Sisters were always the most popular amongst her fellow legions and other organisations that served her God, but Scarlett didn't trust Lady Madeline.

She had to be up to something and Scarlett couldn't figure out what.

This was a simple mission to find the truth about what happened to the sisters in Sanctuary 101. She had to find the sisters, the truth and Jade.

There were no other objectives and Scarlett just wanted to find out what happened to Jade no matter the cost.

Little did Scarlett realise there was going to be a hell of a cost for that knowledge.

CHAPTER 4

Lady Madeline just shook her head at the disgraceful nave as she went away from the heavy steel door and away from the ugly heat that was slowly starting to seep into the nave. The entire monastery was a disgusting sight and deserved no purpose, no function and it certainly didn't help the war effort against the Empire.

The entire religion of the Sirens was a scam.

Lady Madeline stopped in front of a massive perfectly smooth purple wall of sandstone filled with thousands of tiny little handmade candles in the shape of saints and other holy figures. None of the other walls seemed to have these types of candles in their little arches but this wall seemed to be special.

It was strange it was so close to the back of the nave in front of where most of the services and rituals and rites were hell. Lady Madeline just wanted to add it to the rest of her questions about the Sisterhood, but the workmanship was amazing.

Lady Madeline had never seen such incredible tiny details on a small candle before. She could see every single strand of hair, every single pore and eyelash on some of the candles. It was amazing.

"These represent the Sisters that have fallen since the founding of Sanctuary 101," Scarlett said.

Lady Madeline rolled her eyes. She had hoped the damn Sister Superior wouldn't bother her, but they had to get to work at some point and she actually didn't want to be at major odds with Scarlett this early in the mission.

"It's amazing," Lady Madeline said. "I've rarely seen such craftsmanship in my service to Him,"

Lady Madeline turned to look at Scarlett, and she could see the Sister Superior was focused on her. Scarlett was probably trying to size her up, check for any weakness or, more likely, any signs she wasn't devout in her service to the Lord of War.

"I have His authority," Lady Madeline said adjusting her trench coat and blue eye symbol more for effect than anything else.

"That is not my concern," Scarlett said gesturing to her Sisters. "A Black Claw is never sent away from the Divine Lord unless they are on a mission,"

Lady Madeline nodded. Maybe Scarlett was a lot more intelligent than she seemed. Sure she was still a religious nut-job but she had brains.

That was rare to find in the sisterhood.

"So you want to know what my mission is?" Lady Madeline asked noticing some of the other sisters were focusing on them both.

"I do. It is my duty to protect my Sisters and Sanctuary 101. I want to know if you're going to help me or not,"

Lady Madeline gestured they should walk together and after a brief hesitation, Scarlett leant them both slowly across the nave.

"My mission is similar to yours," Lady Madeline said not wanting to lie outright. "It is my mission to find out what happened to the Sisters on Sanctuary. 1000 sisters do not disappear without a trace,"

"You think I do not know that? My own blood sister is included in the missing and everything about this place is odd,"

Lady Madeline forced herself not to smile at the comment about a missing sister. That was good news and hopefully the stupid Sister Superior knows what it's like to lose a sibling but she still wanted to make sure whoever the sibling was, was dead. It was the least Scarlett deserved for what her legion had done to her twin.

"What do you mean everything is odd?" Lady Madeline asked noticing the temperature of Sanctuary 101 dropping even more.

Scarlett stopped and shrugged and gestured to the various sisters around the nave using scanning and equipment.

"We should be able to run scans, detect things and find information on the 1000 sisters that lived here for over a decade. There is no information at all,"

Lady Madeline shook her head. That couldn't be right at all. There had to be something.

"We cannot find a single trace that the 1000 sisters were here at all. It's like every single piece of equipment was delivered here yesterday and never used," Scarlett said.

Lady Madeline smiled because that was a hell of a thing to discover and that made her mission even more interesting. The Sisters were clueless as always, but she didn't want to underestimate Scarlett. She seemed cunning, clever and like she wasn't a typical Siren.

She might even have doubts about the divinity of the Lord of War. A simple fact that made her extremely useful and extremely dangerous.

Lady Madeline just had no idea which side of that line she wanted to put Scarlett on.

No idea at all.

CHAPTER 5

Whilst Scarlett didn't trust Lady Madeline even a fraction of what she could throw her, she didn't want to kill, dispatch or make the Black Claw disappearance just yet. She might actually be useful.

The immense black marble with gold veining Observatory Tower at the very top of the monastery was the real headquarters of Sanctuary 101 where all the weapons, scanners and other pieces of critical technology was located. Scarlett was hardly a fan of the three-hour superhuman-run to get it to and from the nave but given how the lifts and teleporters weren't activated yet, the run was needed.

Scarlett hadn't been to an Observatory Tower for ages and she had forgotten how much she missed it. She flat out loved the wonderful aromas of burning sage, thyme and rosemary that overwhelmed the air so much that only the most devout servants of the Lord of War could possibly enjoy the tower for a long period of time.

She sat in the massive boiling hot steel command throne with thousands of lines of wonderful, holy scriptures carved into the metal when Sanctuary 101 was built. Scarlett liked how the holy words wrapped around her metallic blue armour and it was a great feeling to finally be able to be here in such a holy place.

Jade was probably the last person who sat here and a wave of sadness, anger and grief washed over her a few times. She had to find her sister no matter what and she had to start her mission now.

That was why she had summoned her inner circle.

Scarlett watched her three favourite sisters working away at the various red holographic computer terminals attached to the black marble walls of the tower. She was even more impressed with the designers of the tower than the rest of Sanctuary 101.

The walls might have been curved but the designers had managed to make the curvedness, black marble and the gold vein work together to make a striking depiction of the Lord of War and their legion lord meeting for the first time.

The walls were beyond beautiful.

Scarlett smiled as the overwhelming aromas of rosemary, thyme and sage made the great taste of roast pork form on her tongue and Sister Lydia approached her command throne.

Scarlett had always liked Sister Lydia even though her blue metallic armour was dented, chipped and caked in dirt. She should have punished Lydia for not cleaning her armour more but she didn't want to punish such a devout, trusted and clever Sister.

Lydia was a master of working technological systems so Scarlett just hoped beyond hope that she would know what had happened.

"Sister Superior," Lydia said bowing her head slightly before raising it, "I have finished my analysis of the systems. I have run everything twice and my results are clear,"

Scarlett bit her tongue.

"The systems are exactly the same as they would be as if they were delivered yesterday by the Legion Lord herself. There are no signs of use, no signs of foul play, no signs of anything," Lydia said.

Scarlett stood up. "How is that possible? All records show that Sanctuary 101 was a thriving, powerful convent with over 1000 Battle Sisters. They had to have left a trace of their existence,"

"I do not know my Lady," Lydia said. "I will return to my calculations before the sandstorm hits,"

Scarlett nodded her thanks.

"My Lady," Lydia said before going back to her computer terminal, "if anyone can figure out what has happened here, it is you. The Lord of War would not have sent you if he doubted your ability,"

"Thank you Sister," Scarlett said not wanting to say more in case her voice wobbled.

The very last thing she needed was a sandstorm to hit the convent. She had read enough about the storms of this planet to know that once the storm hit they were completely alone and it would be impossible to get a signal to orbit.

And that concerned her a lot more than she wanted to admit.

"Sister Superior Scarlett," Sister Emilia said in bright, perfect clean armour.

Scarlett smiled at the young Sister who was barely old enough to graduate the Sirens Schools but she was faithful, fierce and Scarlett had a soft spot for her.

"I have checked the armoury on the computer systems and in-person. Everything is exactly as it should be," Emilia said. "My Lady, may I speak out of turn?"

"Of course, Sister," Scarlett said not sure where this was going.

Emilia placed her hands on her hips. "Sanctuary 101 is thought of highly through the Legion and everyone from the lowest Novice to the high ranks of Holy Synagogue, they want to be placed here. Something is very wrong,"

Scarlett couldn't disagree because Sanctuary 101 was the most famous convent in the entire legion. It was the second church the legion ever founded and it's considered the most sacred of all their sites. So what happened here?

"I do not only mean with the computers and the convent itself. I mean the planet, the air and the sounds. This feels too perfect and even though He teaches us to be perfect in His eyes, we all fail to live up to those ideals,"

Scarlett smiled because now the young Sister was walking dangerously close to a cliff. She had known Sister Superiors who would order Emilia to get whipped and tortured hundreds of times for that sentence alone.

But Emilia was right.

Even though Jade was a lot more devout than Scarlett ever wanted to be, she couldn't help but feel that Jade would have made one or two mistakes. Something that they should notice.

Everything was too perfect on this planet.

"I understand your concerns Sister and thank you for speaking frankly," Scarlett said. "Now return to the nave please and join your Sisters for dinner,"

"Thank you Sister Superior and… we are going to find her, you know that right? The Lord of War would not keep us from Jade,"

Scarlett forced herself not to frown and chastised the young Sister for daring to cross that line. She was her Superior and it was improper and rageful for such a young one to talk to her like that.

At least Emilia had been kind so Scarlett just nodded and weakly smiled.

Scarlett looked at the last member of her inner circle, Sister Alice with her bald tanned head and deep black eyes as she smiled at her.

"Sister Superior," Alice said grinning, "I have something,"

CHAPTER 6

Lady Madeline flat out couldn't understand what the hell this convent actually was, what was happening or anything because her own investigation was making no sense. That was why she wanted to find an information relay to hack into.

She went along a perfectly lit and cool pink sandstone corridor with nothing on the perfectly smooth walls. There were no arches, no marks on the ceiling or floor and it was weird how even her metal boots weren't marking the sandstone in any way.

As far as Lady Madeline knew it was why the stupid Sisterhood no longer made their convents or churches out of sandstone or anything besides marble. It didn't happen if marble was native to a planet or not, the Sisters manipulated the atomic structure of a planet to make marble for themselves.

There should have been marks in the sandstone even more so considering a thousand sisters had been living, working and praying here. It made no sense and even the sheer coolness of Sanctuary 101 made little sense.

Lady Madeline opened her long black trench coat a little to allow some of the wonderfully cool air to wrap around her body, given how she had deactivated her disc device an hour before. She had been into the heart of enemy camps, she had assassinated superhumans and she had killed alien monsters, but compared to this mystery, those missions felt easy.

This was not.

Lady Madeline kept going down the long, endlessly straight corridor and everything was only getting cooler. It wasn't cold or icy but it was noticeable.

She got out her small black disc device and activated a setting on it that allowed her to scan the local area in extreme detail. The results weren't exactly anything that surprising, the corridor was made from pure sandstone that got its pink pigmentation from the type of fossils in the rock from millions of years ago.

There were no DNA samples, no signs of anyone had every walked down here and then Lady Madeline scanned for her own DNA.

There was nothing.

She couldn't understand that in the slightest because humans shredded skin cells like no tomorrow. It was why humans were so easy to track, kill and slaughter, so why weren't her skin cells shredding?

Lady Madeline activated another setting on her black disc device and held it just below her arm. She could see thousands of skin cells were shredding every second but as soon as they touched the sandstone floor, they disappeared.

She checked the air quality and it was normal. There was no explanation for what was happening here and that made her smile.

This mystery just kept getting weirder and weirder with each passing hour.

"Lady Madeline," a Sister with a deep voice said.

Lady Madeline rolled her eyes as she turned around and looked at the five approaching Battle Sisters in their bright armour.

"Yes," Lady Madeline said playing with the blue eye symbol around her neck. "Can I help you?"

"The Sister Superior has requested us to find you and bring you to the Service tonight due to begin in an hour. She requires everyone to be there,"

"I am not a member of your church," Lady Madeline said wanting this silly conversation to be over.

"This is not a request," a woman said, her voice low, cold and sharp.

"I am Black Claw and you are interfering with my investigation. Do I have to declare you traitors and excommunicate you from your most holy Church?"

The Sisters took a step back at that comment. Lady Madeline loved how stupid and dumb the sisters were.

"Fine," another woman said but Lady Madeline couldn't see which one, "please be in the nave in one hour,"

"I will do my best," Lady Madeline said giving the sisters a mocking bow as they walked away.

As soon as the sisters were out of sight, Lady Madeline went up the corridor until she found a small metallic blue box attached to one of the walls. It was a standard Angel design so she touched it and her Black Claw DNA opened it for her.

A small red hologram appeared showing her a range of data streams she could click on, but it didn't matter. Regardless of the one she clicked her, every single one of them was blank.

"Black Claw," Lady Madeline said to the hologram. "Enter Code Beta-Omega-Alpha-66, Lady Madeline,"

"Access Granted," the hologram said.

Lady Madeline smiled as she finally had access to the most fundamental pieces of information attached to the computer system. This sort of data was so core and embedded into the system that it was impossible to remove.

She read the limited data stream and she had to admit it was a lot more limited than she normally had access to, but it was enough. She could see the system was first used twelve years ago by Canoness Jade Evans and it was shutdown and a full system wipe was ordered five years ago but the exact same person.

Whatever had happened here Scarlett's sister was

at the heart of it and Lady Madeline was so looking forward to breaking the news to Scarlett.

Her sister might be a traitor to the church and Lady Madeline was so looking forward to seeing Scarlett lose that precious, idealised version of her sister. It would be nothing compared to the pain of losing Charlie but at least Scarlett would suffer a little.

And hopefully there would be a lot more suffering to come.

CHAPTER 7

The overwhelming aroma of burning sage, thyme and rosemary choked out all other hints in the boiling hot Tower, and Scarlett was sure if her and Alice were less devout they would have suffocated on the aroma. A few drops of cold sweat rolled down her back and Scarlett wasn't keen on the loud humming, banging and vibrating of her armour as it worked overtime to cool her down.

The black marble chamber of the Observatory Tower hadn't been this hot earlier. Scarlett had rather enjoyed the coolness of Sanctuary 101 but now it was changing, Scarlett really wanted some answers. The entire convent had seemed cool when they first arrived, which was odd considering none of the technological systems were online.

Now the entirety of Sanctuary 101 seemed to be heating up fast and with the approaching sandstorm, Scarlett really didn't like their odds. If there was a breach in the walls then she wanted to find it as soon as possible so it could be sealed before something worse happened.

"Sister Superior, this is what I found," Sister Alice said.

Scarlett nodded and she focused on the massive tan, bald head of the Battle Sister that still had small scars, slices and dents in it despite the best work of the Healer Sisters. She wasn't sure how many wars and battles Alice had fought in but Scarlett knew it was a lot.

She almost felt lucky to have Alice with her, considering what they might find here but Scarlett just hoped Alice had found something useful.

"What is it?" Scarlett asked leaning over the red holographic computer Alice was working on.

"There is a single system working. Everyone missed it because it isn't even a system we focus on in the sisterhood and no one thinks about it," Alice said.

Scarlett nodded. "Strange but go on. What system is it?"

"Weather Tracking," Alice said letting the statement hang there between them for a moment.

Scarlett didn't exactly know why that was striking. Granted the sisterhood and all Angels of Death and Hope even the Empire ones, mainly focused on weather monitoring as a whole to look at temperature, radiation levels and wind patterns.

That was it.

But from what she could barely remember as her days as a Novice, Weather Tracking Systems were designed to notice patterns over time so reports could be written up, it wasn't a remarkable system in any fashion.

"There were even safeguards installed around the system so when a full-scale reset was activated, the Weather Tracking would survive and keep its data," Alice said.

"Now that is interesting," Scarlett said standing up perfectly straight. "What's so important about the weather of Sanctuary?"

Alice grinned and brought up a geological graph.

"It seems the planet is getting extremely warm," Alice said, "and the Sisters were trying to work out why. Global warming and greenhouses aren't a factor here because of our advance technology and we're the only settlement on the planet,"

"Is that true?" Scarlett asked.

She had asked the question out of instinct but as the overwhelming scent of burning herbs got even more intense, she realised she hadn't questioned that assumption yet. It would make sense for the Sisters to flee and go out into the desert. They would have been wearing their superhuman armour so it was possible.

It was extremely possible to survive in the wasteland if needed, but that still didn't explain the perfect condition of Sanctuary 101.

"I don't think anything could survive this planet," Alice said bringing up another line graph. "This graph shows the number of species over the past twelve years. Over three million species have died out on this planet because of the extreme heat,"

Scarlett gasped. She didn't mean to have such a basic reaction to the news because it was normal for species to die out on planets once they arrived. They hunted down dangerous species to extinction, they purposefully engineered plagues to wipe out certain species and this was normal.

But not on this world and this scale.

"If this extinction event was done by the Sisterhood," Scarlett said, "then all the species would have been dead in the first three years. But most of the species died out in the fourth and fifth year as the planet got extremely hot,"

"Exactly, Sister Superior,"

Scarlett paced around the large black marble tower. She still loved the beautiful walls and how the gold veining was manipulated perfectly to make stunning art in the walls but it only unnerved her now.

Something had happened to this planet, her sisters and Jade and she was only getting more questions rather than answers.

"Can you get the other systems online?" Scarlett asked. "We need the enviro-systems on immediately as well as the long-range scanners?"

"Negative," Alice said grinning. "That's another interesting fact. The enviro-systems aren't online at all. They can't even connect to the computer systems,"

Scarlett rolled her eyes. "Just as if they had been

delivered yesterday,"

"And Sister Superior," Alice said biting her lower lip, "the only other thing I find odd about the computer system is, there are no cleaning bots. No cleaning systems whatsoever. It's like they were never delivered,"

Scarlett laughed nervously. It made no sense that every single other system and piece of technology Sanctuary 101 was here and brand-new except the various cleaning systems. But as much as Scarlett wanted to focus on it, she had bigger problems right now.

Alice nodded. "What do you want me to do?"

Scarlett went to open her mouth because she had a service to prepare for and it was the first time in five years the Sisterhood had returned to one of their most holy sites. But again she had to give Alice new orders because she liked to think the Lord of War would rather have the mystery solved than everyone in a service he would never see.

Scarlett hated she had even had the unholy thought but it was needed. She had to find Jade.

"Reactivate the teleportation and lift systems please. Then I need you to run calculations to check the location of the planet and how it's moved over the past few years,"

"By your will Sister Superior," Alice said bowing her head.

She was seriously starting to hate this mystery but at least she had a lead. She had to learn more about the planet and now she was a lot more interested in its location in the solar system.

The only reason Scarlett could think why the planet was getting even hotter was if the planet was being drawn closer to the sun. It was the only thing that made logical sense but even if that was the case, it still didn't explain what had happened to Jade and all the others.

1000 Sisters were still lost whatever the outcome and that killed Scarlett inside.

CHAPTER 8

Lady Madeline had to admit Scarlett was a seriously clever woman. She liked being a Black Claw because it gave her the tools to have full access to the computer systems of Sanctuary 101 without anyone knowing, whatever Scarlett said near a computer or any of her stupid zealot dogs searched up, she would know.

It was a fascinating idea about the planet moving closer to the sun and she was almost annoyed she hadn't even thought of that. Scarlett was brilliant and as much as Lady Madeline didn't want to kill her in the end, it was simply the way things had to be.

"Sisters, thank you for rejoining me," Scarlett said.

Lady Madeline rolled her eyes, straightened her trench coat and played with her blue eye symbol as she leant against the hot pink sandstone walls at the back of the nave. She had come here to watch the stupid sisters do some kind of ritual and at least it gave her time to do some more hacking.

She had to admit the sisters had done a great job at bringing the nave back to life considering they had only arrived a few hours ago.

All the pink, purple and orange sandstone walls were filled with tens upon tens of thousands of burning handcrafted candles in their little arches. It was stunning and the subtle aromas of burning incense was a nice reminder of the so-called holiness of Sanctuary 101.

She almost believed the Lord of War was a god for a moment. Only a moment though.

"Tonight we honour our brave sisters for their sacrifice, their service and their dedication to Him and everything He does for us," Scarlett said.

Lady Madeline smiled as she looked at the one hundred Battle Sisters standing in the middle of the nave, their bright metallic blue armour shining in the candlelight. They were so glued, so interested and so caught up in Scarlett's words that she didn't doubt she could kill them all before they even noticed.

That was how silly the sisterhood was.

Lady Madeline reached into the left pocket of her trench coat and clicked her disc device and a blue hologram formed over her eyes, though it was impossible for others to see, and she started scanning the room.

She found the exact same as before.

None of the Battle Sisters were wearing their helmets so they were all shredding thousands of skin cells and yet none of them touched the floor at all. It was weird and even their body odour wasn't really registering and she had no idea if their body heat was even registering. The damn nave was so warm, even her device couldn't tell what heat was what.

"So let us preach our Lord and Master's song to refill their holy Convent with the love, joy and protection that He provides us all," Scarlett said.

As the entire nave was filled with the surprisingly sweet, almost moving and emotional singing of the Battle Sisters, she turned her attention to the various computer systems of Sanctuary 101, and thankfully someone called Alice had activated the long-range scanners.

Lady Madeline ran her own scan of the area and made it look like the system had automatically run it for Alice when she reactivated the system.

The scan revealed nothing she didn't already know from the reports the Lord of War had given her on the planet. Everything within a thousand miles of Sanctuary 101 was simply a boiling hot wasteland with sand dunes, a pretend mountain range and more sand than any world had a right to contain.

There were no plants, no water and no signs of life whatsoever.

Sanctuary 101 was the only sign of life on the planet.

"Thank you Sisters," Scarlett said grinning like a little schoolgirl. "It has been far too long since this most holy Convent has been filled with your divine songs. It fills my heart with joy, passion and love for our Lord and Master,"

Lady Madeline rolled her eyes. Scarlett might have been intelligent but she was thick at times. Lady Madeline just had no idea how someone could fall for this rubbish, everyone in the highest levels of the Lord of War's government knew the religion that the Sirens followed was an instrument of control.

Their Legion Lord Luna Kennedy didn't actually believe in the Faith, she only used it to control her legion and others.

The Sisters were beyond pathetic.

The sweet melody of the sisters started up again as they started a brand-new song that made Lady Madeline want to tear her ears off, but she didn't when her device told her about a strange finding in the scan.

Something was coming towards them.

It was a tiny little metal object hidden in the sandstorm but something had registered in the scan.

Lady Madeline tried to get another scan to focus on it but the sandstorm was here.

She closed her eyes and tried to drown out the sweet noise of the Battle Sisters, and she managed to hear the howling, shrieking sandstorm outside.

And her hologram disconnected as the scanners went offline. The sandstorm was simply too much for them to handle.

Now they were blind and it was impossible to get a message to orbit if anything went wrong.

And that excited Lady Madeline a lot more than she ever wanted to admit.

CHAPTER 9

As much as Scarlett had flat out loved the wonderful, delightful, uplifting service and hearing the great voices of her sisters sing out into the void praising their Lord and Master, she hated the constant howling and shrieking of the sandstorm engulfing them.

Scarlett had already sent all the five-women squads around Sanctuary 101 to search, report and repair any breaches but no one reported anything just yet. Sometimes she was worried the sandstorm had brought down the communication system but Alice assured her it was still working.

For all their sakes, Scarlett just hoped that wouldn't change.

She led Sister Emilia down a long, narrow grey granite corridor without any signs of scripture, holiness or love towards Jade's private chambers. The convent might have been one of the most holy places to the Sisterhood but everywhere followed the same patterns. The most senior figure had to sleep in the most uncomfortable chamber as an act of servitude to Him.

Scarlett was really impressed with the sort of questions Emilia had asked her on the way here. Emilia had asked about rising through the ranks, they had even debated scripture and the *real* purpose of the Holy Crusade the Legion Lord was currently preparing for.

Emilia kept saying how much she wanted to be on the Holy Crusade, and Scarlett couldn't blame her in the slightest.

After a few more moments of walking, Scarlett stopped outside a cracked wooden door that led into Jade's chamber. It felt so weird and sickening that she was going to see where her baby sister had slept, worked and prayed to the Lord of War without her here to show her.

It felt like an awful invasion of her privacy and she had no idea what she was going to see. Her eyes watered at the very idea that Jade's corpse was going to be in there, or some reminder that she had lost her precious little sister.

The exact same sister she had read to as a kid, played games with when they were meant to be at school and who she had comforted when their abusers were finished with them after a day of hard labour.

Scarlett's hands formed fists. She hated the Empire and she hated everything they pretended to stand for.

She had to find her sister and she had to continue bringing the Empire one step closer to crashing down around them.

"Sister Superior, are you alright?" Emilia said.

Scarlett smiled and opened the wooden door before she could change her mind.

The overwhelming aroma of oranges, dust and musk filled the air and Scarlett was surprised. This was the first sign that Sanctuary 101 was old she had experienced since coming here hours before.

Scarlett wanted to cover her nose but she forced herself not to. She couldn't show any signs of weakness in front of a young Sister and any discomfort she felt was deserved in her service to Him. She would be okay as long as she kept her Faith.

She went inside Jade's chamber and Scarlett blinked away tears because it looked like Jade had actually slept here.

It was a simple small granite chamber with only a cold stone bed to her left, a stone desk to her right and a scanner and communicator relay in the middle of the chamber.

Thankfully, there was a cracked food synthesiser and mouldy pot of holy oil on the far wall of the chamber. Scarlett just grinned because it was something like this she had been waiting for.

She went over to the desk and there was a large pile of parchment filled with scriptures, sermon ideas and various speeches that was beyond standard for a

Canoness to be writing.

Scarlett was so glad she didn't have to sleep on the stone bed because it looked awful and so uncomfortable. She was happy to experience some discomfort in the name of the Lord of War but a girl had her limits. But the stone bed didn't look like it had been used.

In fact even the stone desk was starting to look new.

"What's happening?" Emilia asked looking at the desk.

Scarlett looked at the desk and her eyes widened as the parchment started disappearing.

"Shut the door," Scarlett shouted.

Emilia slammed the wooden door shut and Scarlett smiled as the parchment stopped disappearing and the overwhelming smell of dust and mould and must returned so strongly it made her cough.

Scarlett was about to say something when her communicator crackled.

"Sister Superior, the top quartile of the convent are secured. No breaches to report," a Sister said.

"Thank you," Scarlett said. "Return to your duties and I bid you a goodnight,"

"That's good news," Emilia said.

Scarlett didn't say anything because she still needed to hear about the lower three quartiles of the convent. And the night was far from over so anything was still possible.

"So," Emilia said pacing around smiling, "what

made the effect stop, Sister Superior? Faith?"

Scarlett was so glad Emilia was smiling when she said that.

"It might be the wood, the granite or some kind of combination?" Emilia asked. "We could run some kind of experiments but I think we should analyse the scene first,"

Scarlett's mouth just dropped. She had no idea the woman was so clever and normal. She was like a breath of fresh air.

Scarlett went over to the desk and flicked through the parchment. One of her favourite things about being a superhuman was her superfast processing speed, she had no idea how baseline humans could tolerate spending hours reading hundreds of pages.

It only took her ten seconds to read, analyse and understand the pages.

Again the parchment was nothing special. It was all standard stuff.

"What if," Scarlett asked, "whatever happened a moment ago was because the parchment was the most recent thing Jade did? For example, the last thing she did was write out and touch the parchment before she left and closed the door,"

Scarlett was certain that's what happened. It was the only thing that made any sense, there had to be some kind of time-distorting thing happening.

"Possible," Emilia said clearly focusing on something else, "but look at this,"

Scarlett went over to Emilia who was standing by the holy oil and she grinned when she saw at the bottom of the pot was a leather journal.

Something Jade had hopefully written in and it was preserved well enough for them to read and understand what the hell was going on.

CHAPTER 10

"You shouldn't be here,"

Lady Madeline just smiled and shook her head at poor stupid Sister Alice as she stood up from her holographic computer terminal in the Observatory Tower.

She just couldn't understand why the pointless sisterhood was so obsessed with manipulating the black marble and its gold veining to produce such interesting but futile depictions. The command throne was nice enough but Lady Madeline was looking forward to destroying everything the sisterhood stood for.

Lady Madeline coughed at the foul choking aroma of damn burning rosemary, thyme and sage. It was way too much and she wanted to find where the smell was coming from and blow it up. It was insane how the Battle Sisters could enjoy that foul aroma for so long.

Alice pulled her gun up. Lady Madeline laughed

at the silly Sister, she didn't doubt Alice would shoot her given the chance and she had no doubt the explosive rounds of the gun could kill her.

Yet Lady Madeline wasn't going to let Alice shoot her because she was a silly little zealot and she was a Black Claw.

"Stand down," Lady Madeline said pointing to the blue eye symbol around her neck and straightening her trench coat. "I have the authority here and you need to tell me the results of your calculations,"

Alice stood up perfectly straight. Lady Madeline forced herself not to react to the sheer height difference between herself and the superhuman. Something she hadn't noticed until now.

"I will do no such thing. The Sister Superior must hear my results first and the calculations haven't even been completed yet,"

Lady Madeline rolled her eyes. "I am a Black Claw, a servant of your Lord and Master and I communicate with him directly most days. You are a mere servant of His Church and you are interfering with my Holy work,"

She wanted to laugh at the faithful rubbish she was saying but Lady Madeline just wanted to see how easy to manipulate the dumb Sister actually was.

"Let me talk to my God," Alice said.

Lady Madeline grinned. All the Sirens were so easy to manipulate, control and she was amazed the Lord of War actually respected the Legion as much as he did.

"Of course," Lady Madeline said, "but first tell me what your calculations show at the moment,"

Lady Madeline reached a hand into her right pocket and pulled out something that looked like a small twig that was actually a holo-dagger. A small flick of her wrist and she would have a dagger that could slice through anything.

And poor stupid Alice would be dead.

"Of course," Alice said gesturing Lady Madeline to come over to her screen. "I accounted for galactic shift and I ran every single calculation I know and it seems that nothing strange has happened. The planet is still exactly where it is meant to be given the natural shift of the galaxy,"

Lady Madeline folded her arms. "Thank you, but that doesn't account for the extreme heat of the planet,"

She was really glad she had her small disc device in her pocket as she noticed Alice had a large drop of sweat running down her forehead and into her cold black eye.

"You seem to be clever," Lady Madeline said hating she was admitting a Sister could be smart. "What might be causing the planet's heat?"

Alice paced around for a few moments then she clicked her fingers and smiled.

"Do you know about the Runaway Greenhouse Effect and The Ideal Gas Law?"

Lady Madeline smiled because that was a brilliant

idea, and very clever for a Sister.

"Yes," Lady Madeline said. "The Runaway Greenhouse Effect confirms that when a planet has a large enough amount of greenhouse gases like water or carbon dioxide in its atmosphere, the planet's temperature increases,"

"Exactly my lady," Alice said. "Then this increase in temperature causes even more water and greenhouse gases to enter the planet's atmosphere, causing even more solar radiation and heat to be trapped within the planet. Making the temperature increase even more,"

Lady Madeline gasped as everything was starting to make sense.

She had read the reports earlier about how no one could go outside Sanctuary 101 without protective equipment because of they would simply boil away. Even the superhuman Sirens were struggling with the heat.

"Then," Alice said, "this increase in temperature and changes in air composition leads to increases in pressure so the temperature only increases more. The Ideal Gas Law proposes that if pressure increases without a correction then the temperature does too,"

Lady Madeline wasn't exactly sure that was the precisely correct definition for the Ideal Gas Law but her physicist of a father would have been proud. She couldn't kill Alice painfully for knowing something her father would have respected her for.

In fact, Lady Madeline really didn't want to kill

Alice at all because she was clearly brilliant. Yet her mission was simple, she couldn't allow the Sisterhood to find out the truth behind this planet and what had happened to the sisters of Sanctuary 101.

She was almost tempted to keep Alice alive because she didn't feel like the Runaway Greenhouse effect and the Ideal Gas Law explained what was happening completely. She just didn't want to believe Sanctuary had enough greenhouse gases on its own to produce such a violent effect.

She almost believed someone else had increased the amount of greenhouse gases on the planet artificially, and Alice might be great help in figuring out who that person was.

But her mission was still clear.

Lady Madeline went over to Alice and hugged her.

"Thank you and now I'll let you talk to your God,"

Lady Madeline flicked her wrist and the holo-dagger shot into Alice's chest piercing both her superhuman hearts.

Alice collapsed herself the floor and her eyes widened in horror as the corpse disappeared and boiled away in front of her.

CHAPTER 11

Scarlett felt so wrong, confused and shocked that she was invading a Canoness's personal journal. The wet, oily leather felt weird with its coolness and sticky hardness as the holy oil dripped off the leather cover and splashed onto the granite floor.

She was a little surprised at how well-preserved and perfect the parchment pages were, but that was the benefit of Faith. Scarlett didn't doubt that with enough pray and sacrifice the Lord of War could and would do anything for his servants. Especially servants as great as Jade was.

Emilia's faithful humming was a little off-putting but Scarlett rather liked the sweet, uplifting melody that gently echoed off the granite walls. It was a melody normally reserved for battles but Scarlett supposed it was okay given they had no idea what was happening.

"What does the journal say my Lady?" Emilia asked.

Scarlett shrugged, and she stopped herself. She was a Sister Superior, it was bad enough she was allowing a young Sister that was still basically a novice to talk without permission, let alone know the personal contents of a Canoness's journal.

But if anyone could help her find her precious little sister, Scarlett knew it was Emilia. She was smart, devout and clearly capable of thinking for herself.

She needed someone like Emilia now more than ever.

"It's mainly just scripture, her thoughts on what different passages meant. She talks about her favourite lines, religious figures and the weather. It seems she stopped writing, she was writing essay after essay on the weather of the planet,"

"Why?"

"I don't know," Scarlett said smiling. "If I knew that I would know where my sister was, but she's being extremely methodological. Each of these essays ranged from five thousand words to twenty thousand words and some include empirical formulas and data,"

Emilia cocked her head. "Permission to speak freely my Lady,"

Scarlett nodded knowing roughly what she was going to say.

"Canoness Jade Evans was devout as they come and she was an extremist in the eyes of some within our Holy Order. The notion she would include empirical equations and data would… could she have been opening her mind or losing her Faith?"

Scarlett bit her tongue so hard she felt the warm metallic taste of blood fill her mouth before her superhuman biology sealed the wound a second later. She hated how Emilia was accusing her sister of being unfaithful but it wouldn't have been a bad thing for Jade to become less blinded to the truth of the universe.

Science was the foundation of the universe and the truth that their Faith was built on. Without science there would be no superhumans so no Lord of War and in turn, no Faith.

"I agree," Scarlett said. "A lot of her early essays were looking at the weather through a theological perspective then as time went on each essay turned more and more empirical in nature drawing on different disciplines until she believed she had cracked open the problem,"

"Then what?" Emilia asked.

"The essays stop, so clearly Jade wanted to keep exploring her ideas and incorporate her essays together but something stopped her,"

Scarlett went over to her sister's cold stone bed and sat on it. The coldness was a delightful change from the extreme heat of the planet but something else was going on here. Her sister believed she had figured it out but Scarlett couldn't understand the essays.

They were too random, too scrambled and

sometimes a little to advance for her.

"Sister Superior, the second and third lower quartiles are secure," a Sister said over the communication network.

"Thank you. What about the fourth quartile that covers the lowest 25% of Sanctuary 101's structure?" Scarlett asked.

Static filled the line for a moment.

"My Lady, we cannot reach Sister Mira. She was coordinating the five squads of Battle Sisters inspecting those levels," a woman said.

Scarlett shook her head. This was the last thing she needed but the howling and shrieking of the sandstorm outside got a lot louder and Scarlett's stomachs churned violently.

"Secure the entrances to the fourth quartile and wait for my arrival. Summon the Black Claw too, she should be here for this," Scarlett said wanting to make sure it wasn't Lady Madeline killing her people.

"What are we going to do about this?" Emilia asked gesturing to the room.

Scarlett rolled her eyes. As soon as she opened the wooden door whatever was happening here would devour the room again and annihilate any trace that her sister had ever been here.

She flicked through the pages of the journal one more time and committed it to her superhuman memory just in case she had missed anything the first time. Then she looked around the chamber a final time.

It was incredible to think that her precious baby sister had slept, worshipped and had run an entire convent from this room. She was amazing and Scarlett couldn't be prouder of her wonderful sister.

Now she just had to find what had happened to her but she couldn't help but have a sinking feeling that something had just joined them. And something had just come in from the storm.

She didn't know how she knew that, but she just did. Maybe it was word from her Lord and Master or maybe it was just knowing how things always got worse before they got better.

CHAPTER 12

Lady Madeline felt disgusting as a small bead of sweat rolled down her back. She was a Black Claw, she had access to some of the most advanced technology the galaxy had ever seen and she was still sweating like a primitive ape. It was wrong and foul and just disgusting.

Lady Madeline went towards Sister Superior Scarlett and her twenty Battle Sister strong escort wearing their helmets. Only Sister Emilia and Scarlett weren't wearing their helmets which was a little odd considering Emilia was only a young Sister but Lady Madeline didn't care too much. She had to complete her mission and get her revenge on the Sisterhood.

They all stood in the lowest levels of Sanctuary 101 made from bright, vivid blue, yellow and pink strips of sandstone and granite that connected to the wasteland outside.

The corridor was hot, musty and so dry that Lady Madeline flat out hated it with its dirty yellow walls.

The only nice thing about it was there were no silly faithful symbols that plagued the rest of Sanctuary 101.

Lady Madeline couldn't stop thinking about the metal object she had picked up on the long-range scans.

They weren't alone on this planet and that concerned her. Not scared her because Black Claws never felt fear but it concerned her.

Each of the sisters in the bright metallic blue armour stood firm with their long fingers on the trigger of their guns filled with explosive rounds.

She didn't exactly like her odds if the Sisters decided to turn their weapons on her, but she did like a challenge. And she had already killed silly Alice, so a few more dead Sisters would hardly matter.

The odd taste of desert felt wrong in her mouth as Lady Madeline could have sworn her throat felt bone dry and like all the moisture in her body was trying to escape. Maybe it was and maybe the planet was finally getting too extreme to support any type of life.

Even superhuman life.

"What have you found?" Lady Madeline asked.

Scarlett just stared at her and Lady Madeline was glad she still had the small holo-dagger in her hand just in case.

"Twenty Battle Sisters are missing. There are no traces of their armour, their DNA and there's no damage to any of the structures," Scarlett said.

Lady Madeline looked at each of the Battle Sisters who were slowly raising their guns at her. She played with her trench coat a little and blue eye symbol again to remind them of who she was.

The Battle Sisters kept raising their weapons.

Another concerning fact if there ever was one.

"The problem is that the bodies are dissolving quicker than you would ever believe," Lady Madeline said coldly.

Everyone raised their guns at her and she grinned. The Battle Sisters were so predictable.

"That is typical," a Battle Sister said. "It is typical that the Black Claw will withhold information from us. She is a heretic against the Lord of War and she is impeding in our Holy Mission,"

Lady Madeline couldn't tell which Battle Sister had said it but it was good to know there were some stupid brainwashed fools still here. They were the easiest to kill.

Scarlett whipped out her own gun as did Sister Emilia and they both aimed at Lady Madeline's head.

As much as Lady Madeline didn't want to believe they were good shots, from everything she had seen, read and observed about the Sister Superior, she had no reason not to doubt her skill.

"What haven't you told me?" Scarlett asked.

Lady Madeline looked around. She had twenty guns focused on her from all different angles from different Battle Sisters with different levels of experience and accuracy. She also had a Sister

Superior who was a little emotional and she had a weakness of her little sister Jade.

Those were not bad odds, but Lady Madeline just wanted to see what would happen if Scarlett knew the truth.

So she told Scarlett, Emilia and the other Battle Sisters about killing Alice and what she had found out before her death.

"Heretic!" a Battle Sister shouted.

A Sister aimed her gun.

Lady Madeline threw the holo-dagger so quickly and strongly that it exploded into the Sister's chest.

The entire corridor broke out into gasps, shouting and faithful muttering until they all watched the Sister's corpse fall onto the floor and it simply boiled away and disappeared.

"That is what happened to Sister Alice," Lady Madeline said. "That is what will happen to all of us if we are not careful and there is something else,"

Scarlett came straight over to Lady Madeline, so close that the Black Claw could feel Scarlett's warm dry breath on her face.

"What aren't you telling me?" Scarlett asked.

"She hasn't told you about me," a voice said.

CHAPTER 13

As soon as Scarlett heard the voice she spun around and pointed her gun in the direction of the words. All the other Battle Sisters did the exact same motion but stupid Lady Madeline only stood there like she was at the cinema.

She was surprised when she saw at the other end of the corridor was someone standing in the dirty metallic blue armour of the Sisterhood. Scarlett couldn't tell the rank, Order or anything else but she knew that armour anywhere.

They were standing in the presence of a fellow Sister but something felt off.

Scarlett had met thousands of Battle Sisters and something wasn't right. The entire Legion regardless of their Order all shared the same vibes, the same posture and the same everything. They were a single united holy blade that would smite His enemies.

This Battle Sister lacked all of that.

The figure or Sister took a step towards them

and Scarlett hated how slightly odd it was. The step was almost like a stumble or it looked like a child was just learning how to walk for the first time.

Scarlett licked the inside of her mouth. It was bone dry and she felt like her throat was closing up on it and the humming, banging and vibrating of her armour trying to keep her cool was deafening.

Scarlett could barely hear herself think as she realised every Battle Sisters' armour was straining to keep them cool.

"What are you?" Scarlett asked aiming for a headshot on the figure.

"The Black Claw did not tell you about me that is interesting. Why do you think she hid that from you? Is it because mission to kill you all?"

Scarlett's eyes widened. She had never trusted Lady Madeline, there had always been something off about her and it made sense.

Scarlett fired her gun.

The explosive round smashed into the figure's head and it went down.

"I might not trust her but I trust her more than you," Scarlett said turning to look at the Black Claw. "And you better not be hiding anything more from me,"

"Of course not," Lady Madeline said grinning.

"Sister Superior," Emilia said as she was nearing the corpse.

Scarlett rushed over to her and made sure Emilia didn't do something stupid and touch the body.

But there wasn't a body.

Scarlett shook her head as she inspected the shattered shards of the metallic blue armour. This had definitely once belonged to a Battle Sister but there was no sign of anyone or anything inside the armour.

"Why did this armour survive and 999 other sets did not?" Scarlett asked.

"How do you know they didn't?" Lady Madeline asked coming over too.

Scarlett rolled her eyes. She really didn't want to have to deal with even more lifeless pieces of armour attacking and trying to confuse them.

And then it hit her.

Scarlett looked at Emilia and Lady Madeline. They were the only two Battle Sisters here that didn't have their helmets on.

Emilia and Lady Madeline both gasped and Scarlett just grinned because she had fucked up badly. When she had come down here she had just met the Battle Sisters like they were meant to be here.

Because she had ordered them down here because these were the Battle Sisters led by Sister Mira. They weren't missing, she was standing around them.

"When I killed that Battle Sister who tried to kill me," Lady Madeline said, "I didn't see any flesh. I only saw the armour dissolve,"

"Me too," Emilia said.

All the fake Battle Sisters laughed manically around her so much that the sandstone started to shake and vibrate and small chunks collapsed around them.

The temperature shot up.

Scarlett's armour banged a final time.

The cooling systems were destroyed.

Sweat tried to pour off her.

But Scarlett just collapsed as the heat engulfed her and her world went black.

CHAPTER 14

When Lady Madeline opened her eyes again, she just laughed as she felt perfectly cool, almost cold and she gripped the thick metal chains around her wrists. She was hanging over a massive sandstone pit and she had to admit it was a great time to be alive.

Lady Madeline couldn't see the bottom of the pit but the rough, razor-sharp edges of the pit made her grin a little more. She seriously didn't want to fall into the pit because she was sure even she might die. There was a chance Scarlett could survive it because she seemed to be the type but she still didn't want to test it.

The large pink sandstone cavern she was in smelt awful with the foul aroma of burning sage, thyme and rosemary like that damn observatory tower. Lady Madeline wanted to find where the bloody burning herbs were and destroy it.

She hated the smell almost as much as she hated the Sirens.

"It's good that you're awake," a voice said in the darkness of the cavern.

Lady Madeline stayed silent. She had been captured once or twice before and the key was always to remain silent and force your enemy to react first and tip their hand.

"You want to be strong I am guessing. That is typical for Black Claws, you see Sister or Canoness Jade knew a lot about your organisation,"

Lady Madeline forced herself not to react to that revelation. The Black Claws were meant to be mysterious and deadly and surrounded by mystics. She didn't want some pathetic faithful nutter to know much about her.

"Jade had even studied you especially. You were special she thought and she believed you could be a great addition to her ranks,"

Lady Madeline so badly wanted to laugh at the stupidity of that comment, she would rather die than join the Sirens. Then she realised that wasn't what the voice actually said. The voice had only mentioned "her ranks", it never said about the ranks were.

"I can feel your interest interesting," the voice said.

She shook as she felt like bugs were running around her skin and crawling through her hair. Lady Madeline wanted to highlight her blue eye symbol and straight her trench coat as something to comfort her but she didn't have them.

Lady Madeline looked into the darkness of the

cavern and noticed they were both on a small wooden table close to the edge of the pit.

"You have no power here Black Claw," the voice said changing its tone to become hyper-feminine. "This domain belongs to me and no one will change that. Not the Church, not the Battle Sisters and not you,"

Lady Madeline smiled because the voice had revealed something that made the Lord of War's hints make a lot more sense now.

"Alien," Lady Madeline said. "It is the only explanation that makes sense. The Lord of War said the Empire wasn't involved, no one could know the truth and the Lord of War needed to be kept clean,"

The voice laughed. "If I was an alien why would that impact the Lord of War?"

"Because he would have sent his own holy servants onto an inhabitant world without telling them on purpose. He sent them here to die and that would have massive implications for the Church. It would be a political nightmare, not a death sentence to the Church but it would make converting the faithless more challenging,"

Lady Madeline noticed a shadow move in the darkness and she hissed as the metal chains got even colder.

"You are wrong Black Claw," the voice said stepping into the light.

The voice was still wearing the bright metallic blue armour of the Sirens but it was headless. The voice didn't have a helmet and that unnerved her more than she ever wanted to admit.

"I am not an alien," the voice said. "I am something far more impressive,"

Lady Madeline screamed as she felt thousands of bugs and insects crawl all over her skin and in her hair.

She watched as hundreds of tiny metal scarabs climb out of the armour and towards her.

Lady Madeline felt the scarabs crawl up her hair and onto the metal chains.

"Goodbye Black Claw," the thousands of scarabs said as one.

The chains snapped.

Lady Madeline fell into the darkness.

CHAPTER 15

Scarlett gasped as she landed in a small, deep pool of mouldy, musty holy oil. The taste of mouldy roasted pork formed on her tongue and once she rose to the surface, the air smelt awful with hints of rotting flesh, rosemary and fetial matter filling the air.

She climbed out the awful pool and just shook her head at the bright light out above her from where she had fallen from only moments ago. She hated those scarabs but at least things were starting to make sense.

"Sister Superior," Emilia said.

Scarlett looked around the large rocky cavern made from black granite and noticed there were two other holes in the ceiling so presumably Emilia and maybe even Lady Madeline had fallen down too.

"Over here," Emilia said.

Scarlett followed the voice in the pitch darkness and frowned when she found Sister Emilia sitting against the rough granite walls. Her leg armour was twisted, mutilated with muscles and bones shooting out in all directions.

"The Healer Sisters will help you, just have Faith," Scarlett said knowing she was lying.

Emilia was going to die here. She didn't want to lose another Battle Sister, much less someone who was clever, brilliant and able to think beyond the dogma of the Sisterhood.

Scarlett couldn't allow Emilia to die, not if she could help herself.

"The Lord of War wanted you here Sister Superior. He has faith in your power, your skill and your dedication. He will guide you to your purpose and he has guided me to mine," Emilia said.

Scarlett smiled and she looked around for anything she could use, but the cavern was empty. It was only the two of them, the twisted pools of holy oil and the granite stone.

Even if she had the tools to make some kind of climbing pins, the granite would be impossible to hammer them into, even with her superhuman strength.

Someone else splashed into another pool.

Scarlett rushed over to the pool and folded her arms when Lady Madeline's head breached the surface. She was half tempted to push her back down but the Black Claw looked strange without her trench coat and blue eye symbol.

Lady Madeline actually looked a little powerless, weak and normal. Not that Scarlett was going to underestimate the woman for a single moment, but that might be exactly what they needed right now.

"Tell me you have something," Scarlett said offering the Black Claw a hand up.

She was surprised when Lady Madeline took it and Scarlett pulled the other woman up.

"Negative," Lady Madeline said. "The Voice or whatever those things are took my coat and my symbol. I'm nothing without them,"

"Throne," Scarlett said. "We can't be that powerless between us, and we have to figure out a plan. There are at least 80 Battle Sisters still alive in Sanctuary 101. I am not letting them die,"

"Have Faith," Emilia said weakly.

Scarlett rushed over to her. Emilia's face was ghostly white and it was clear even her superhuman biology wasn't keeping her alive.

She was not letting Emilia die.

"You must have some skill," Scarlett said to Lady Madeline. "You're a bloody Black Claw. Aren't you all-powerful? Capable of burning entire planets and turning them inside out,"

Lady Madeline folded her arms. "Not without my equipment. Without my gadgets, I'm just me. Extremely deadly but I don't know how to get us out of this situation,"

Scarlett laughed and she slumped herself against the sheer heat of the granite walls. She hated to imagine how hot it was outside given how hot it was deep underground.

After everything she had done, all the prays, all the sacrifice and all the killing she had done to get the honour of leading the expedition to find Jade; she had failed. Scarlett had failed to find her precious little sister who was so much better than her.

Maybe Jade was exactly what she needed.

"We're going to die here," Lady Madeline said.

Scarlett laughed and she stood up perfectly straight, placing her hands on her hips. She looked at the granite cavern and she noticed this had to be made by the Sisterhood. There was a craftsmanship and plenty of tiny little symbols and carvings in the very edges of the ceiling.

Her Sisters had made this cavern so there was hope.

"We need to get out of here," Scarlett said.

"How?" Lady Madeline asked.

"By using the words of our Lord and Master obviously,"

Scarlett grinned as she felt her faith, her power and all her Sisters fill her body. She felt the strongest and most powerful she had in years because she had the faith. She was going to burn this entire planet to the ground if her faith required it because she was done messing around.

Her Sisters, her Church and Jade needed her.

Scarlett went to the centre of the cavern and knelt, bowing her head slightly.

"Oh bloody hell," Lady Madeline said rolling her eyes.

"Oh shut up," Scarlett said. "I need quiet and if you do not give me that I will kill you myself for disrespecting His will,"

Lady Madeline folded her arms and zipped her mouth shut.

Scarlett nodded her thanks and she closed her eyes.

"Dear Him on Terra, I bid you to leant me some of your holy strength this day and your wisdom. I do not ask this out of selfishness but so I can be guided to the purpose you have laid out before me,"

"Oh my god," Lady Madeline said.

Scarlett smiled when the Black Claw hissed in pain so hopefully Emilia had thrown something at her.

"Lend me your power and show me the way out of here so I can smite your foes and bring us all one step closer towards the death of the Empire, the alien and the mutant. All shall die before your righteousness,"

A loud humming filled the cavern and Scarlett opened her eyes and smiled. A small section of the granite wall was lifting up revealing a steel ladder stinking of rosemary and incense.

"Grab her," Scarlett said to Lady Madeline pointing to Emilia. "No sister gets left behind,"

Scarlett didn't even wait for a response. She marched over to the ladder and started climbing.

She was going to find these scarabs and she was going to make them pay for despoiling and attacking the Sisterhood.

Even if it was the last thing she ever did.

CHAPTER 16

Lady Madeline had heard rumours of the power, sparkles and mysterious happenings of the sisterhood but this was amazing. She had no idea how deep below Sanctuary 101 they were as they went along a long, wide solid steel corridor but it was impressive.

Scarlett led them with her fists out in front of her and she was humming, singing and muttering prays as she went. Each so-called holy act made the corridor hum and buzz and pop with light and power.

Lady Madeline had heard a few of her organisation propose that the sisterhoods had installed small things to do when certain words were said, but whatever was going on, it was impressive to watch.

It almost made her feel hopeful.

"Have Faith," Emilia said quietly.

Lady Madeline rolled her eyes as she continued carrying the injured Battle Sister on her back. Even without her leg armour, she still weighed a ton and

Lady Madeline would have preferred her dead but Scarlett had been firm.

No more Sisters are dying here.

"Over here," Scarlett said going over to a circular door and opening it with a passcode.

They went inside and the sheer stink of the incense made Lady Madeline's eyes watered and the extreme heat of the room made her head hurt.

After a few moments Lady Madeline noticed they were back in the cavern where she had been hanging over the pit. The small wooden table was there so Lady Madeline put on her trench coat and blue eye symbol.

A scarab chomped into her flesh and Lady Madeline screamed in utter agony as she felt one of the icy cold metal creatures crawl into her body and make its way towards her brain.

"Help!" Lady Madeline shouted.

"Oh Throne," Scarlett said rushing over.

Scarlett ripped open Lady Madeline's arm and grabbed the creature but then it multiplied and even more scarabs entered Lady Madeline's flesh.

Lady Madeline screamed in crippling pain. Her entire body felt like it was on fire and her vision blurred from the pain. She couldn't focus, she couldn't hear.

She only screamed.

She collapsed to the ground.

Then everything went silent and she couldn't feel or see Scarlett anymore. She was still inside the cavern but there wasn't a door anymore and she felt cold.

It felt wonderful after the past hours but she broke out into a fighting stance because something wasn't right here.

"You can relax you know," a voice said echoing all around her. "I've only hijacked your audio-visual processing areas of your brain. It was simple really. That's what I love about humans,"

Lady Madeline went to speak but her mouth wasn't working.

"For a species that is so messy and ugly, you are rather easy to control. I just wished you weren't so messy,"

Lady Madeline managed a gasp as everything fell into place around her and everything made perfect sense considering what she had overheard Sister Alice say to Scarlett about the lack of cleaning systems.

The scarabs were the cleaning systems.

It explained why Sanctuary 101 was so perfect, so spotless and everything was brand-new, because the cleaning system had been tasked to keep it that way.

Lady Madeline couldn't exactly understand what had happened or gone so wrong because she had never heard of this happening before. Normally on warships, military bases and normal worlds loyal to the Lord of War, the enviro-systems regulated and cleaned every single hour.

Sometimes more.

Of course nanobots were used a lot of the time because they were fun and they doubled as security measures.

She had never seen scarabs before.

"And so she works it out. Oh you humans are delightfully clever at times but you are still messy. Messiness is bad. Dirt is bad. Humans are bad," the voice said.

Lady Madeline noticed the mechanical edge to the tone now and she felt like she could speak again.

"You learnt something from Jade and the other Battle Sisters didn't you?" she asked.

"Of course we did. Our programming is firm. We have to keep Sanctuary 101 sterile and clean and you are the biggest threat to that mission so you have to die,"

"So you studied the Battle Sisters, infected them and studied their brains," Lady Madeline said knowing these cleaning scarabs were probably based on some new type of nanobot weaponry.

Hence the infecting and self-learning function.

"Affirmative," the voice said. "We noticed the Sisters were a threat so we tried to kill you all easily enough. The Runaway Greenhouse Effect was a good idea at first. The Sisterhood had already imported twice the amount of water naturally found on the planet so we boiled it away,"

Lady Madeline nodded. She had found that some nanobot weaponry could superheat itself to kill the host and melt its brain. She had no issue believing these scarabs could do the same to water.

Then she realised that a scarab was right inside

her brain so it could kill her at any moment.

"You are an idiot," Lady Madeline said knowing it was the first thing that popped into her head.

"Maybe but I need you to tell me how do I get into orbit?"

Lady Madeline smiled because the scarab had finally revealed what it truly wanted more than anything else in the galaxy. It wanted to escape Sanctuary and it probably wanted to sterilise the rest of the galaxy.

And as much as Lady Madeline wanted to destroy the sisterhood she just couldn't allow that to happen.

Too many innocent lives would be lost.

She had to stop these scarabs even if that meant saving the Sirens.

CHAPTER 17

A loud deafening hum and the sound of hundreds of thousands of tiny metallic legs crawling over stone filled the cavern as Scarlett reached into Lady Madeline's pocket and grabbed a holo-dagger.

She hated how there were thousands of tiny scarabs climbing down from the ceiling and they were slowly coming towards her, but they weren't storming her just yet. She didn't know why but she didn't care.

It gave her time and that was all she needed.

It made sense these scarabs were part of a new cleaning system that the Sisterhood had been testing out here but it had gone extremely wrong. Scarlett understood that and she accepted that without question but she wasn't sure how to stop them.

"Sister," Emilia said.

Scarlett rushed over to Emilia and slashed a scarab that was about to crawl into her neck.

The scarab shrieked in pain as it died. All the other scarabs stopped probably running some kind of analysis through their systems.

Scarlett noticed the temperature was warm here but it wasn't boiling. And she tried to figure out the temperature other times she had seen the scarabs.

She wanted to believe that the scarabs could survive anything but she knew that wasn't true. Even when the extreme heat had knocked her out, the scarabs had been inside the armour of her Sisters. Armour especially designed to keep her cool but maybe it still kept the scarabs cool enough without the cooling systems.

The scarabs were vulnerable to the extreme heat.

That was what she needed to do.

Ten scarabs dropped down on her.

Scarlett let her training take over.

She lashed. Slashed. Sliced the enemy.

The scarabs stopped their advance again but Scarlett didn't doubt they would just storm her after a few moments.

Scarlett knew Sanctuary 101 wasn't that different from all the other standard monasteries of the Sisterhood. They all had their weak points and they had extremely good ventilation systems that could flood a floor or entire building with hot or cool air or even toxic air.

She had to flood Sanctuary 101 with extreme heat and just hope beyond hope that her and her Sisters survived it.

It was the only way.

A loud humming filled the cavern and all the

scarabs turned away from Scarlett and hundreds of thousands of metallic legs banged over stone as they crawled away.

Scarlett went to throw her holo-dagger when she felt someone stare at her.

She spun around and noticed Lady Madeline's body was staring at her but her eyes were so cold, distant and dead that Scarlett knew *this* wasn't Lady Madeline.

"All your sisters will be cleansed," Lady Madeline said. "Just like I have always wanted you murdering bitches,"

Scarlett slammed her fist straight into the woman's jaw and she charged towards the door.

She didn't want to leave Emilia but she had to flood the building and that meant she had to ask the Lord of War for permission again.

Something she doubted the scarabs would allow her to do.

Scarlett left the cavern and ran as fast as she could up the solid steel corridor without any of the wonderful holy symbols of her Sisterhood.

She muttered holy words, prays and melodies and after a few moments bright sparkles of red, blue and purple light rained down from the ceiling.

Her Sisters were with her and her faith endured.

A deafening shirk ripped through the corridor.

Scarlett spun around. Thousands of scarabs were chasing her. They were too fast for her.

Scarlett kept running.

She saw the empty armour of a Battle Sister up ahead. She grabbed it. Checked it was clear and she put on the helmet.

Sealing it up tight.

Scarlett knelt on the floor and hissed as she felt the thousands of scarabs pour over her.

They tackled her to the ground and the sound of tens of thousands of metal legs clawing away at her armour was deafening.

Scarlett activated the amplifiers inside the helmet and she prayed.

"Lord of War give me your strength to smite your enemies on this day. Open all the ventilation systems and flood this most holy Sanctuary with the outside air to slay your foes,"

Nothing happened.

Scarlett felt like she was getting crushed. Almost as if a house had landed on her.

"I do this as your faithful servant. I do this to kill your foes like always and I do this to help you my most holy Lord,"

Scarlett screamed as she felt her leg armour buckle, crack and smash open. The scarabs let out a massive cheer of delight.

"I sacrifice myself every day for you my Lord. Help me!" Scarlett shouted.

The scarabs stopped for a brief moment and then they chomped onto her flesh and Scarlett screamed and screamed and screamed as crippling pain flooded her body.

Then the howling and shrieking of the raging sandstorm filled the corridor and the Scarabs screamed themselves in terror.

The temperature shot up and Scarlett ripped off her armour so the scarabs had nowhere left to hide.

As the heat engulfed her she just hoped her faith would protect her.

Scarlett's world went blurry before the heat claimed her and her world went black.

CHAPTER 18

For the past two days, Lady Madeline had been learning everything she possibly could about what had happened when the scarabs had invaded her mind, body and brain. She was impressed with Scarlett and everything she had done, and it had explained what had happened to her.

All Lady Madeline remembered a deafening metallic shriek as the scarabs raced out of her body to find cool ground. Yet it didn't work and the scarabs died, not that it helped her much as she collapsed bleeding and battered.

Thankfully with the sandstorm clearing up, the Battle Sisters in orbit had launched a search party and they had found their kin in the upper levels of Sanctuary 101 okay and well. So all forces had turned their attention to the lower levels where Scarlett, Emilia and Lady Madeline were.

Thankfully Emilia was alive too and she even had new mechanical legs so she could walk, fight and pray like nothing had ever happened.

Lady Madeline respected her for that, because only in death did duty end.

She held her cool black trench coat under her left arm and she held her blue eye symbol in her hand as she stared at the recovering, burnt body of Sister Superior Scarlett. It was clear the Sister Superior was incredible and could survive anything.

And Lady Madeline was actually glad about that.

As much as Lady Madeline didn't want to admit it, the nave was actually rather pretty considering the Sisterhood had created it, and the Healer Sisters were using it as a base of operations.

The only problem was the damn awful smell of incense, oranges and rosemary that choked out all other smells in the nave. Lady Madeline was looking forward to never smelling that mixture ever again.

The massive sandstone walls in all their different colours were sort of stunning in a weird sort of way, and the thousands upon thousands of arches were skilful, clever and Lady Madeline supposed the Sisters who had designed and executed this nave deserved her highest respects.

The nave really was that stunning.

Lady Madeline was a little surprised she didn't want to blow up or burn Sanctuary 101 down anymore. She actually enjoyed looking at all the little people-shaped candles in the arches in the walls with their precise and awe-inspiring details.

She had wondered if the candles represented all

the Sisters lost here in Sanctuary 101, and she was glad she had scanned each candle a second and third time to confirm a small suspicion she had only realised she had had after the discovery of the Scarabs.

Lady Madeline was never going to tell the Sisterhood this but she had compared the image of each candle against each member of the Sirens on the planet. There was a candle for each of them and there was only a single set of DNA on each of them. At first she wasn't sure why the scarabs had allowed the DNA mess to remain on the candles but Jade had touched each of them.

She had probably crafted them herself and maybe it was her pure faith that protected the candles that honours her fallen sisters against the predations of the scarabs.

Lady Madeline wasn't sure but it was a nice enough thought, and it had meant she didn't need to focus on her real mission for a little bit longer. Now she had to make a decision.

She needed to either kill Scarlett or leave her alone.

The choice had to be made.

Scarlett was laying on a metallic blue hovering medical bed with a small medical device attached to her chest that showed tens upon tens of different data streams that were moving way too fast for her baseline human eyes to process, but it probably meant tons to the Healer Sisters.

When the Healer Sisters and other reinforcements had arrived down from orbit, the Healer Sisters had converted the nave into a medical wing whilst they treated the injured. Lady Madeline had allowed the awfully fussy Sisters to heal her and help to loosen her joints after the torture of the scarabs but she didn't thank them.

Or maybe she did by not killing them. If her organisation learnt how she had allowed herself to be tortured by the scarabs then maybe she would have been demoted or worse. She just hoped that wouldn't happen.

Lady Madeline flicked her holo-dagger between her fingers and just smiled because this was a hard choice. A damn hard choice to make.

Lady Madeline went over to Scarlett's bedside and looked at the sleeping Sister Superior, because she knew everything now and everything that had happened on Sanctuary. She knew what had happened to her sister Jade, her fellow Battle Sisters and she knew how the Lord of War had made a mistake.

He had personally commissioned the scarabs and they had gone wrong, extremely wrong. Lady Madeline had checked her databases and with her friends in other organisations about the scarabs and they had never been used again.

The Lord of War had known his mistake and kept it. He had never shared it with the Sisterhood, Scarlett or anyone who deserved to know. And

Scarlett wasn't stupid enough not to figure it out.

Sooner or later she would work out that the Lord of War was to blame for all of this and she could do so much damage to the war effort against the Empire.

Or would she?

Lady Madeline pressed the cold edge of the twig-like device that housed the holo-dagger against Scarlett's forehead. It would only take a small flick to activate the weapon and kill the Sister Superior.

But Scarlett was too good for that.

She was devout in her own special way, she was going to do whatever it took to kill the Empire and guide humanity towards the iron grip of the Lord of War. Lady Madeline didn't want to rob His forces of that kind of power.

So her mission was done.

Lady Madeline placed the holo-dagger back in her pocket and she grinned. She had completed her mission because she had discovered the truth behind Sanctuary 101 and she just had a feeling that Scarlett wasn't going to tell anyone the truth.

She was too clever, too tactical and too faithful at heart to risk insulting her Lord and Master. So Scarlett wasn't a risk to the Lord of War so his hands would be kept clean.

And as much as Lady Madeline wanted to punish the Sisterhood for killing Charlie, she felt like the Sisterhood had already suffered enough. The Sirens had lost 1000 of their stupid kin five years ago, they had lost at least another 20 two days ago and Scarlett had lost a blood sister.

That was enough suffering. It really was.

Lady Madeline kissed Scarlett on the forehead and she left Sanctuary forever.

Later on Scarlett would question how, when or why Lady Madeline left but there would be no record and no one would ever remember seeing her leave the planet or escape orbit.

But she did.

It was simply how Black Claws worked and Lady Madeline loved her life, her job and she loved completing her mission.

CHAPTER 19

Two days later, Scarlett just grinned as she leant against the wonderfully cool and refreshing yellow sandstone wall that was completely repaired. She had ordered the walls to be repaired and all the slashes, lashes and chunks to be removed, and she was still impressed beyond words.

That was the power of the Lord of War, the Sisterhood and her faith. Scarlett was so proud to be a Siren of Ares because she had access to technology and slave workers that most humans could only dream about.

The smooth sandstone wall felt refreshing against her back armour and there were no more lumps, bumps or shards of sandstone trying to stab her unlike a few days ago. And the air was no longer trying to kill her, Scarlett really liked the warming hints of oranges, lemons and limes that clung to the air as Sanctuary 101 was finally being blessed all over again.

Every single millimetre, room and candle in the convent was being covered in holy oil once more, and the distance singing and laughing of her Sisters as they shouted out holy melodies and prays at the top of their superhuman lungs, just made Scarlett grin like a little schoolgirl.

This was exactly what the Sisterhood stood for and Scarlett loved it.

Scarlett stared out over the endless yellow wastelands and she was glad there were no more dunes, no more mountain-sized piles of sand and everything was perfectly flat. It was an endless wasteland of yellow sand but that was perfect.

The blue sky was crystal clear with only a handful of clouds in the distance, and Scarlett seriously enjoyed not having to put up with the constant humming, vibrating and banging of her newly repaired armour trying to keep her cool.

Sanctuary had been restored.

Two days after she had been rescued by her Sisters and worked on by the Healer Sisters, Scarlett had ordered the nearby Forge Worlds to send terraforming equipment to her location immediately. She didn't complain that it had taken a day instead of weeks, thanks to some kind of new Slideway technology they had invented recently.

Scarlett had loved watching the Terraformers get to work on restoring the planet's natural balance. She had never seen so much water, carbon dioxide and other greenhouse gases being pulled out of an atmosphere before, but it was possible. And now those greenhouse gases could be weaponised against the Empire.

All helping the Legion Lord's Holy Crusade against the Unfaithful.

Scarlett was glad the Forge Worlds had also sent over brand-new and non-psychotic cleaning systems that had finished being installed yesterday. They were already cleaning the convent perfectly and not a single Sister had died, but she still knew the truth.

The Lord of War was to blame for this.

If the Lord of War, her Lord and Master, had simply admitted his mistake about developing the cleaning scarabs instead of hiding the fact from the Sisterhood. Then so much trouble and potential death could have been avoided.

Yet she understood it.

Scarlett wasn't blind to the internal politics of the Anti-Empire Legions. Even her own Legion Lord, like the other 4, were plotting how to gain power for themselves so they could rule the legions for themselves. It would only take a major mistake to make the Lord of War lose power and then everything would change.

And the Empire might survive.

As much as Scarlett didn't want the Lord of War to escape, Scott-free given how his mistake had cost the life of her little precious sister, Scarlett didn't want him gone. He was her Lord and Master after all and her entire life was based on the idea that Him, and

Him alone, was in charge and the rightful ruler of humanity.

She couldn't oppose him. And she was fairly sure if she kicked up too much of a fuss then she would be killed anyway and that would only serve the Empire even more.

Scarlett wanted the Empire to die no matter the cost.

She had already written two versions of her final report, one containing the absolute truth that she sent to her Legion Lord personally, and the other a much watered-down version of the truth that blamed the Empire wholeheartedly.

But she had kept out a single thing from both reports.

She hadn't included why the nanobots and the scarabs had been unable to touch Jade's bedchamber until the wooden door was opened. It had taken her days to figure out what had happened but Scarlett had worked it out. It was Jade's sheer faith in the Lord of War that had protected the space.

Scarlett had read about quantum entanglement and how the right action potential (or thought) and the right wave function had the power to have a physical impact in the material universe. Scarlett didn't doubt Jade had no idea what she was doing, but all Jade wanted in the entire galaxy was to be protected by her Faith.

So Scarlett didn't doubt that after years and years of studying, praying and being consumed by her

Faith. She had hit something in the universe and all her wishes had come true, and as long as the chamber was sealed, her Faith protected her.

Until the wooden door was open and the seal was broken.

"Sister Superior," Emilia said coming over to her and joining her leaning against the wall. "You have a message from the Lord Of War Himself and our Legion Lord,"

Scarlett took the small blue disc Emilia offered her and Emilia was about to walk away when Scarlett placed a gentle hand on her shoulder.

"Read this with me, Sister Superior," Scarlett said knowing Emilia had more than earned the promotion.

Scarlett activated the disc and Legion Lord Luna's voice poured out.

"Sister Superior Scarlett is dead, you are now Mother Superior and you must return immediately to the Holy Synagogue so we can confirm your new appointment. You are needed in the Holy Crusade. We trust you to appoint a worthy Sister to lead the convent in your permanent absence,"

Scarlett smiled and frowned and then smiled again as the message stopped.

She had never dreamt of being a Mother Superior before, that would mean she would be in charge of entire solar systems that the Sisterhood operated in. She was going to be one of the most powerful Sisters in the Legion, but she would never allow herself to rise above the Sisterhood.

The Legion was everything and a united legion was the only thing that would ensure the Empire's death.

Scarlett hugged Emilia. "Then this is where I leave you Sister Superior, you are clever, you are bright and you know when to follow and when to question our doctrines. I cannot think of a better person to lead one of our most holy convents,"

Emilia tightened the hug a little before breaking it and she knelt for her superior one last time.

Scarlett nodded her thanks and then she summoned a shuttle. There was a lot of work to do against the Empire to ensure that the Lord of War ruled humanity with an iron fist, but that was all tomorrow's problem.

Her mission was here and she had discovered what had happened to the 1000 Sisters of Sanctuary 101 and her precious little sister. And now, Scarlett was going to make Jade even prouder because she was going to join the Holy Crusade and fight side by side with their Legion Lord and maybe even their God.

And if that wasn't a sensational ending to a mission then Scarlett never wanted to know what was, because life was far too brilliant, wonderful and positive for her to want it spoiled for any reason at all.

GET YOUR FREE SHORT STORY NOW!
And get signed up to Connor Whiteley's newsletter to hear about new gripping books, offers and exciting projects. (You'll never be sent spam)
https://www.subscribepage.io/garrosignup

About the author:

Connor Whiteley is the author of over 60 books in the sci-fi fantasy, nonfiction psychology and books for writer's genre and he is a Human Branding Speaker and Consultant.

He is a passionate warhammer 40,000 reader, psychology student and author.

Who narrates his own audiobooks and he hosts The Psychology World Podcast.

All whilst studying Psychology at the University of Kent, England.

Also, he was a former Explorer Scout where he gave a speech to the Maltese President in August 2018 and he attended Prince Charles' 70th Birthday Party at Buckingham Palace in May 2018.

Plus, he is a self-confessed coffee lover!

Other books by Connor Whiteley:
Bettie English Private Eye Series
A Very Private Woman
The Russian Case
A Very Urgent Matter
A Case Most Personal
Trains, Scots and Private Eyes
The Federation Protects
Cops, Robbers and Private Eyes
Just Ask Bettie English
An Inheritance To Die For
The Death of Graham Adams
Bearing Witness
The Twelve
The Wrong Body
The Assassination Of Bettie English
Wining And Dying
Eight Hours
Uniformed Cabal
A Case Most Christmas

Gay Romance Novellas
Breaking, Nursing, Repairing A Broken Heart
Jacob And Daniel
Fallen For A Lie
Spying And Weddings
Clean Break

Awakening Love
Meeting A Country Man
Loving Prime Minister
Snowed In Love
Never Been Kissed
Love Betrays You
Love And Hurt

Lord of War Origin Trilogy:
Not Scared Of The Dark
Madness
Burn Them All

Way Of The Odyssey
Odyssey of Rebirth
Convergence of Odysseys
Odyssey Of Hope
Odyssey of Enlightment

Lady Tano Fantasy Adventure Stories
Betrayal
Murder
Annihilation

Agents of The Emperor
Deceitful Terra
Blood And Wrath

Infiltration
Fuel To The Fire
Return of The Ancient Ones
Vigilance
Angels of Fire
Kingmaker
The Eight
The Lost Generation
Hunt
Emperor's Council
Speaker of Treachery
Birth Of The Empire
Terraforma
Spaceguard

The Rising Augusta Fantasy Adventure Series
Rise To Power
Rising Walls
Rising Force
Rising Realm

The Fireheart Fantasy Series
Heart of Fire
Heart of Lies
Heart of Prophecy
Heart of Bones
Heart of Fate

<u>City of Assassins (Urban Fantasy)</u>
City of Death
City of Martyrs
City of Pleasure
City of Power

<u>Lord Of War Trilogy (Agents of The Emperor)</u>
Not Scared Of The Dark
Madness
Burn It All Down

<u>Miscellaneous:</u>
Dead Names
RETURN
FREEDOM
SALVATION
Reflection of Mount Flame
The Masked One
The Great Deer
English Independence

OTHER SHORT STORIES BY CONNOR WHITELEY

<u>Mystery Short Story Collections</u>
Criminally Good Stories Volume 1: 20 Detective Mystery Short Stories
Criminally Good Stories Volume 2: 20 Private Investigator Short Stories
Criminally Good Stories Volume 3: 20 Crime Fiction Short Stories
Criminally Good Stories Volume 4: 20 Science Fiction and Fantasy Mystery Short Stories
Criminally Good Stories Volume 5: 20 Romantic Suspense Short Stories

<u>Connor Whiteley Starter Collections:</u>
Agents of The Emperor Starter Collection
Bettie English Starter Collection
Matilda Plum Starter Collection
Gay Romance Starter Collection
Way Of The Odyssey Starter Collection
Kendra Detective Fiction Starter Collection

<u>Mystery Short Stories:</u>
Protecting The Woman She Hated
Finding A Royal Friend
Our Woman In Paris

Corrupt Driving
A Prime Assassination
Jubilee Thief
Jubilee, Terror, Celebrations
Negative Jubilation
Ghostly Jubilation
Killing For Womenkind
A Snowy Death
Miracle Of Death
A Spy In Rome
The 12:30 To St Pancreas
A Country In Trouble
A Smokey Way To Go
A Spicy Way To GO
A Marketing Way To Go
A Missing Way To Go
A Showering Way To Go
Poison In The Candy Cane
Kendra Detective Mystery Collection Volume 1
Kendra Detective Mystery Collection Volume 2
Mystery Short Story Collection Volume 1
Mystery Short Story Collection Volume 2
Criminal Performance
Candy Detectives
Key To Birth In The Past

All books in 'An Introductory Series':
Clinical Psychology and Transgender Clients
Clinical Psychology
Moral Psychology
Myths About Clinical Psychology
401 Statistics Questions For Psychology Students
Careers In Psychology
Psychology of Suicide
Dementia Psychology
Clinical Psychology Reflections Volume 4
Forensic Psychology of Terrorism And Hostage-Taking
Forensic Psychology of False Allegations
Year In Psychology
CBT For Anxiety
CBT For Depression
Applied Psychology
BIOLOGICAL PSYCHOLOGY 3RD EDITION
COGNITIVE PSYCHOLOGY THIRD EDITION
SOCIAL PSYCHOLOGY- 3RD EDITION
ABNORMAL PSYCHOLOGY 3RD EDITION
PSYCHOLOGY OF RELATIONSHIPS- 3RD EDITION

DEVELOPMENTAL PSYCHOLOGY 3ʳᵈ EDITION
HEALTH PSYCHOLOGY
RESEARCH IN PSYCHOLOGY
A GUIDE TO MENTAL HEALTH AND TREATMENT AROUND THE WORLD- A GLOBAL LOOK AT DEPRESSION
FORENSIC PSYCHOLOGY
THE FORENSIC PSYCHOLOGY OF THEFT, BURGLARY AND OTHER CRIMES AGAINST PROPERTY
CRIMINAL PROFILING: A FORENSIC PSYCHOLOGY GUIDE TO FBI PROFILING AND GEOGRAPHICAL AND STATISTICAL PROFILING.
CLINICAL PSYCHOLOGY
FORMULATION IN PSYCHOTHERAPY
PERSONALITY PSYCHOLOGY AND INDIVIDUAL DIFFERENCES
CLINICAL PSYCHOLOGY REFLECTIONS VOLUME 1
CLINICAL PSYCHOLOGY REFLECTIONS VOLUME 2
Clinical Psychology Reflections Volume 3
CULT PSYCHOLOGY
Police Psychology